Dear Parents:

Congratulations! Your child is taking the first steps on an exciting journey. The destination? Independent reading!

STEP INTO READING® will help your child get there. The program offers five steps to reading success. Each step includes fun stories and colorful art or photographs. In addition to original fiction and books with favorite characters, there are Step into Reading Non-Fiction Readers, Phonics Readers and Boxed Sets, Sticker Readers, and Comic Readers—a complete literacy program with something to interest every child.

Learning to Read, Step by Step!

Ready to Read   Preschool–Kindergarten
• big type and easy words • rhyme and rhythm • picture clues
For children who know the alphabet and are eager to begin reading.

Reading with Help   Preschool–Grade 1
• basic vocabulary • short sentences • simple stories
For children who recognize familiar words and sound out new words with help.

Reading on Your Own   Grades 1–3
• engaging characters • easy-to-follow plots • popular topics
For children who are ready to read on their own.

Reading Paragraphs   Grades 2–3
• challenging vocabulary • short paragraphs • exciting stories
For newly independent readers who read simple sentences with confidence.

Ready for Chapters   Grades 2–4
• chapters • longer paragraphs • full-color art
For children who want to take the plunge into chapter books but still like colorful pictures.

STEP INTO READING® is designed to give every child a successful reading experience. The grade levels are only guides; children will progress through the steps at their own speed, developing confidence in their reading.

Remember, a lifetime love of reading starts with a single step!

*A special thanks to the wonderful people of
the Pacific Islands for inspiring us on this
journey as we bring the world of* Moana *to life.*

Copyright © 2017 Disney Enterprises, Inc. All rights reserved. Published in the United States by Random House Children's Books, a division of Penguin Random House LLC, 1745 Broadway, New York, NY 10019, and in Canada by Penguin Random House Canada Limited, Toronto, in conjunction with Disney Enterprises, Inc.

Step into Reading, Random House, and the Random House colophon are registered trademarks of Penguin Random House LLC.

Visit us on the Web!
StepIntoReading.com
randomhousekids.com

Educators and librarians, for a variety of teaching tools, visit us at RHTeachersLibrarians.com

ISBN 978-0-7364-3684-7 (trade) — ISBN 978-0-7364-8197-7 (lib. bdg.) — ISBN 978-0-7364-3685-4 (ebook)

Printed in the United States of America
10 9 8 7 6

Disney

M@ANA

Pua and Heihei

adapted by Mary Tillworth

based on an original story by
Suzanne Francis

illustrated by the Disney Storybook Art Team

Random House 🏠 New York

It is feast day!
Moana finds a shell.
She will make a gift
for her dad!

Pua the pig
wants to help.

Moana makes
a shell anklet.
She hears a noise.
Heihei the rooster
has a coconut stuck
on his head!

Moana pulls
off the coconut.
Heihei pecks the sand.
Silly rooster!

Villagers get ready
for the feast.
They wrap food
in leaves.
Heihei pecks holes
in the leaves!

A plate sticks
to Heihei's foot.
He is making a mess!
Gramma chases Heihei.

Gramma slips!
Moana catches her.
But the anklet falls
onto Heihei's neck!

Gramma grabs
a basket.
She runs after Heihei.

Gramma traps Heihei
in the basket!
Heihei pecks
the basket.

Gramma will keep Heihei
in the basket
until after the feast.

Moana's anklet is lost!
Pua the pig sees it
in the basket.

Pua will get it back.

He puts the basket

on a stick and jumps.

The basket flies!

But it does not open.

Pua has another idea.

He ties seaweed

around the basket.

Pua runs fast.

The basket bounces.

But it does not open.

Pua tosses the basket
into a tree.
He jumps up
onto a branch.
The branch bends back.

The branch
springs forward.
Pua and the basket fly
through the air!

Pua and the basket land.

Thump!

The basket opens!

Pua and Heihei roll

across the sand.

They roll
into a fishing net.
They are trapped!

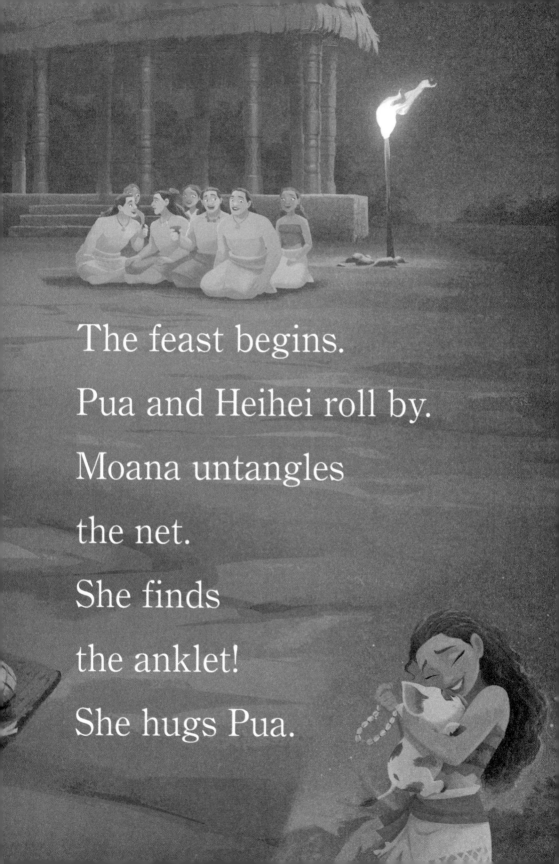

The feast begins.
Pua and Heihei roll by.
Moana untangles
the net.
She finds
the anklet!
She hugs Pua.

Moana's dad
loves his gift!
Heihei walks
into the basket again.
Silly rooster!